THREE OF CUPS

A SHORT, FRIENDS TO LOVERS, FOUND FAMILY,
TAROT ROMANCE

TAROT FANTASIES
BOOK THIRTEEN

JAX WILDER

THREE OF CUPS

Tarot Temptations Series

RAINBOW QUARTZ PUBLISHING

Three of Cups © 2024 by Jax Wilder

Published by Rainbow Quartz Publishing

Edmonds WA, 98026

ISBN: 978-1-961714-64-9

First Edition: 2024

Cover design by Miranda Townsend

Interior design by Miranda Townsend

Library of Congress Cataloging-in-Publication Data has been applied for.

This book is a work of nonfiction. Names, characters, places, and incidents are either the product of the author's imagination or used fictitiously. Any resemblance to actual events, locales, or persons, living or dead, is entirely coincidental.

For permissions or inquiries, please contact:

Rainbow Quartz Publishing at rainbowquartzpublishing@gmail.com

For Amanda

3 OF CUPS

"Let us raise our cups high in celebration, as we dance in harmony and embrace the beauty of togetherness," 3 of *Cups.*

KEY WORDS AND PHRASES:

Celebration and joyous gatherings
Friendship and camaraderie
Reunion with loved ones
Shared happiness and mutual support
Socializing and bonding with others
Emotional fulfillment and contentment
Expressing gratitude and appreciation
Festivities and good times
Community and belonging
Harmonious relationships and connections

The Three of Cups is a symbol of celebration—it's all about coming together with friends and having a good time.

Picture a moment of celebration, three cups raised in a toast to happiness and friendship. There is a sense of delight and enthusiasm that arises when you are surrounded by the people you hold dear.

Celebrating the good things in life is important, so don't forget to take the time to enjoy them. It's a gentle reminder that it's good to unwind and have a good time every now and then.

However, what's important to note is that the Three of Cups is not solely about partying. It also represents the significance of connection and friendship. Surround yourself with people who lift you up and make you feel good.

When The Three of Cups card appears in a reading, it serves as a gentle reminder to value your friendships and savor the moments of joy that come into your life. Life is a party, get ready to dance!

—Lorelai Hamilton, author of *Teenage Tarot* and *Tarot Tales & Magic Spells*

CHAPTER
ONE

The Arcane Room was even more enchanting than I'd imagined. Shelves groaned under the weight of ancient books, crystals caught the light in mesmerizing glints, and the scent of incense wound through the air like a gentle caress. I took a deep breath, trying to ground myself amid the chaos of color and mystery. My fingers skimmed over a deck of tarot cards with the illustration of two women entwined, lips just a whisper apart.

"Interesting choice," a voice murmured from behind me. I turned, and there stood Ms. Vesper, her silver hair cascading in waves down her shoulders, eyes gleaming like she knew every secret I was hiding. She glanced at the deck in my hands, her lips twitching into a wry smile. "Drawn to that one, are you?"

"Couldn't resist," I replied, holding up the deck. "It's got a certain... vibe."

She let out a soft chuckle. "You've got good instincts. That deck is special. Interested in a reading?"

I shrugged, feigning nonchalance though my pulse had quickened. "Why not? I've never had a reading like this before."

Ms. Vesper's eyes twinkled. "Then today's your lucky day."

With a graceful sweep of her hand, she led me to a dimly lit alcove at the back of the store, where the walls were covered in tapestries embroidered with symbols I couldn't quite place. She pulled a deck from a polished wooden box and began to shuffle it, her hands moving with practiced ease. Her rings glinted under the light, a curious mix of silver and moonstone. She laid the deck out in a fan, the cards whispering softly against each other as they spread out before me.

"Pick one," she instructed, her gaze unwavering.

I slid my fingers over the cards, letting them brush against my skin until one practically hummed beneath my touch. When I pulled it from the deck and flipped it over, the Three of Cups stared back at me—three women, laughing, their cups raised high as if in celebration of something unseen.

Ms. Vesper leaned in, her voice low and warm. "The Three of Cups is about connection, friendship... shared joy. But this version has a twist," she said, her gaze shifting back to me. "It hints at boundaries stretched and maybe a little bit more."

"Sounds... interesting," I murmured, barely able to tear my gaze from the card.

Her smile grew, as if she could read the thoughts tumbling through my head. She handed me a steaming cup of tea, the scent of honey and lavender rising to meet me. "Drink this. Then, make yourself comfortable in the room through that door. Let whatever happens, happen."

I moved to the door, finding myself in a small, white-walled room with only a leather chaise lounge in the center. I hesitated but sat down, the cool leather beneath me a stark contrast to the warmth spreading through my body from the tea. Ms. Vesper's eyes met mine one last time before she closed the door with a soft click.

As I sipped, a pleasant heaviness settled over me. My limbs grew warm and heavy, and before I knew it, my eyelids fluttered shut.

When I awoke, the room was silent and still, as if no one had been there at all. Ms. Vesper had vanished, leaving only the faint scent of her perfume lingering in the air. I stood, stretching, and tried to shake off the strange fog clouding my mind. The place was deserted, as if everyone had simply vanished. I called out a quiet, "Thank you," to the empty air and stepped out into the sunlight, breathing in the crisp morning air.

The coffee shop across the street beckoned like a beacon. I needed caffeine, something to jolt me back to reality. The familiar scent of roasting beans wrapped around me as I stepped inside, the quiet hum of conversation and clinking cups grounding me.

As I waited for my order, I felt a pair of eyes on me. Turning, I met the gaze of a woman perched at a nearby table, stirring her coffee lazily. She was striking—short black hair that framed her face in a way that made her cheekbones look like they could cut glass, and eyes so intense they seemed to see right through me.

"Long night?" she asked, a slow smile spreading across her lips.

I raised an eyebrow, trying to match her energy. "You could say that. And you? What brings you here this morning?"

She leaned forward, resting her chin on her hand, her eyes never leaving mine. "I was just passing through, but I'm glad I stopped. I don't usually meet someone quite as... intriguing."

I laughed, feeling a flush creep up my neck. "Intriguing, huh? That's one way to put it."

She stood up, taking her cup with her, and moved to the counter beside me. "I'm Sam," she said, her voice a rich purr that sent a shiver down my spine.

"Spencer," I replied, my voice a little breathless.

Her gaze dropped to my lips, and then back up to meet my eyes. "Spencer. I like that." Her hand brushed mine as she reached for a napkin, the contact sending sparks up my arm. "You feel like doing something a little... unconventional?"

I arched a brow, intrigued. "I might be up for that."

She nodded toward the back of the shop, where a narrow hallway led to the restrooms. Without a word, she turned and sauntered down the hallway, glancing back once to make sure I was following. My heart pounded as I slipped into the bathroom behind her, locking the door with a soft click.

Before I could catch my breath, her hands were on my waist, pulling me close as her mouth claimed mine. She kissed me like she had something to prove, her lips firm and demanding, her fingers digging into my hips as if she couldn't get enough.

I gasped as she lifted my leg, bracing it on the sink. Her hand slipped beneath the hem of my dress, fingers tracing the curve of my thigh as she pressed me against the wall. Her mouth found my neck, nipping lightly, sending bolts of heat through me.

Her hand slid higher, under my dress, finding the wetness between my folds, and I couldn't help the moan that escaped me. She smiled against my skin, her fingers slipping inside, teasing and coaxing until I was dizzy with need. Her thumb circled my clit, applying just the right amount of pressure, while her other hand pressed gently against my throat, not choking, just holding.

"God, you're so hot," she murmured, her voice a low rasp that made my knees weak. She continued her relentless teasing, each touch sending me higher until the tension finally snapped. I bit down on her shoulder, muffling my cry as the waves of pleasure washed over me.

When it was over, she stepped back, a satisfied smile playing on her lips. She licked her fingers, savoring the taste with a wink. "Thanks for the morning pick-me-up," she said, smoothing her dress as if nothing had happened.

I leaned against the sink, trying to catch my breath, but she was already gone, leaving me breathless and reeling, wondering how I'd ever explain this to anyone.

CHAPTER

TWO

As I stepped out of the coffee shop, a lingering smile played on my lips, and the morning sun was just starting to warm the sidewalk. I'd barely gone half a block when I heard familiar laughter behind me. I turned, and there they were—Addison and Riley, my best friends since forever, arm in arm, strolling toward me with matching grins.

"Well, well," Riley drawled, her dark eyes twinkling as she took in my flushed cheeks. "Somebody looks like they've been up to no good."

I couldn't help but laugh, feeling that familiar mix of excitement and comfort that always came when they were around. "Let's just say I've had an... interesting morning."

Addison, with her blonde waves and the kind of

curves that made you want to give her an appreciative once-over, wrapped an arm around my shoulders, pulling me close. "Sounds like you have a story to tell. But first—how about a sleepover? Just like old times. My place. Tonight."

"A sleepover?" I echoed, feeling a rush of nostalgia hit me. I hadn't had a real slumber party since... well, probably since high school. The idea had a certain pull to it, a kind of magic that only seemed possible when we were all together.

"Exactly like old times," Riley chimed in, slipping her hand into mine. Her fingers wove through mine in a way that felt surprisingly intimate. I looked down, a flutter stirring in my stomach as I remembered how I used to daydream about moments like this, imagining the softness of her skin against mine, our hands intertwined. It felt natural—maybe even too natural.

I squeezed her hand, savoring the warmth of her palm against mine. "I'm in. Let's grab a few things from my place first."

We walked together, Riley's hand still in mine, Addison on my other side, close enough that our shoulders brushed with every step. I felt surrounded, cocooned between them, like we were slipping back into an old rhythm, something we hadn't shared in years.

The walk back to my apartment wasn't long, but they filled it with laughter and little teasing glances that kept my heart racing. Every now and then, I'd catch Addison's gaze lingering on me, a subtle spark in her blue eyes that sent a shiver down my spine. I couldn't tell if I was imagining things or if there was something different in the air today, something charged with possibility.

As we reached my door, Addison leaned against the frame, arms crossed over her chest, giving me an appraising look. "So, tell us about this 'interesting morning' of yours. Don't think we're letting you off that easy."

I fumbled with my keys, grinning at her. "Well, let's just say I met someone in the coffee shop. She was... confident. We might have ended up in the bathroom together."

Addison's eyes widened, and Riley let out a low whistle. "You saucy minx! And here I thought you'd just been catching up on sleep," Riley said, nudging me with her shoulder.

I laughed, shaking my head as I pushed open the door. "It wasn't exactly planned. But she made a move, and, well... I didn't exactly resist."

"Spence, I'm impressed," Addison said, a smirk tugging at the corners of her mouth. She brushed her hand down my arm, her fingers lingering just a moment too long. "You're full of surprises today."

My cheeks flushed as I led them inside, trying not to overthink the way Addison's hand had lingered on my skin. I grabbed a bag from my bedroom and tossed in a few essentials while they hovered around, inspecting the books stacked on my nightstand and teasing me about the state of my closet.

Riley picked up a framed photo of the three of us from our high school days, her smile softening as she traced a finger over the glass. "God, look at us. Feels like another lifetime, doesn't it?"

Addison joined her, the two of them standing so close their arms brushed. "We were such babies back then," she murmured, her voice a little wistful. She looked up, catching my eye. "But some things don't change. I'd still follow you two anywhere."

There was a spark in her gaze that made my pulse skip. I wondered if she felt it too, this crackling tension that seemed to simmer just beneath the surface today. I'd thought about them this way before, of course—little daydreams, fleeting fantasies that I usually brushed off as nothing more than wishful thinking. But here we were, just the three of us, and the air between us felt almost electric.

I shook my head, forcing myself to focus as I zipped up my bag. "Okay, I'm ready. Let's get this slumber party started."

As we headed out, Addison took my bag and slung it over her shoulder, her hand finding the small of my back as we walked. "So, this woman... was she as hot as you?" she asked, her voice teasing.

"Oh, hotter," I replied with a grin, feeling a rush of warmth as she laughed and nudged me.

Riley's fingers brushed mine again, and this time, she slipped her hand back into mine, holding it as if it were the most natural thing in the world. I looked over, and she flashed me a knowing smile, her thumb tracing light circles against my skin. It sent a thrill through me, and I wondered if she could feel my pulse quicken under her touch.

The rest of the walk to Addison's place was filled with their questions, playful and a little prying, and the laughter that bubbled up between us felt like a warm blanket wrapping around my heart. I couldn't help but think back to those high school nights, when we'd pile onto a bed, share secrets in hushed whispers, and promise we'd be friends forever.

Inside, Addison's apartment was cozy and welcoming, with soft lighting and an inviting couch that looked perfect for curling up on. She set my bag down by the door, and Riley kicked off her shoes, making a beeline for the kitchen. "I'll get the wine," she called over her shoulder. "You get the blankets. We're doing this right."

Addison met my gaze, a mischievous glint in her eye. "You heard the lady. Get comfy."

I followed her into the living room, feeling a twinge of excitement as I watched her move, so sure of herself, so at ease. I wondered if they had any idea how many nights I'd spent wishing I could tell them how I really felt, how many times I'd imagined what it would be like to hold their hands, to feel their skin against mine.

The night was just beginning, and with every touch, every glance, I felt the boundaries between us start to blur. I could only hope they were feeling it too.

CHAPTER
THREE

The lights were low, casting a warm glow over Addison's living room as we sprawled across the floor, blankets and pillows piled around us. The air smelled like melted chocolate and the rich, tangy aroma of red wine. I took a sip, savoring the way it lingered on my tongue, and tried to ignore the little thrill that ran through me every time one of them brushed against me.

"So," Addison began, pulling a blanket around her shoulders and nudging Riley with her foot. "What movie are we starting with? I'm in the mood for something fun. Something we haven't seen in a while."

Riley tilted her head, her eyes brightening. "How about *The Craft*?" She grinned at me, her eyebrow quirking up in that way that always made my heart skip. "Remember when we were obsessed with it?"

I laughed, remembering late nights spent huddled around the TV, wide-eyed as we watched those girls cast spells and cause chaos. "Oh, absolutely. I think we might have all tried levitating each other at least once."

Addison chuckled, raising her glass in a mock toast. "And we failed spectacularly. But I'm down. I haven't seen it in ages." She glanced over at me, her gaze lingering. "Or maybe we go with something more... romantic. Like *10 Things I Hate About You.*"

Riley let out a dramatic sigh, rolling her eyes. "Oh god, the number of times you watched that movie." She shot me a mischievous look. "Remember when we were watching it, and you and Addy disappeared for, like, half an hour?"

I felt a blush creep up my cheeks, recalling exactly what had happened. Addison and I had been fourteen, the air heavy with that adolescent mix of nerves and excitement. We'd snuck away under the guise of grabbing snacks, but it hadn't been food we were after.

Addison's laughter was a little softer now, and she leaned over, brushing a strand of hair from my face. "It was a long time ago, but I remember." She glanced between me and Riley, her smile turning a little sad. "Spence, you ever think about that kiss?"

My heart raced as the memory surfaced—a stolen moment in the dark, her lips on mine, soft and sweet. I'd thought about it more times than I'd ever admit, wondering if it had meant as much to her as it had to me. "You... you remember that?"

She nodded, taking a deep breath. "I remember everything about that night. I also remember pretending it didn't happen the next day, which, looking back, was probably the worst thing I could have done."

Riley, who had been listening quietly, leaned back, watching us with a thoughtful expression. "Why did you pretend it didn't happen, Addy?"

Addison sighed, her gaze dropping to her lap. "I don't know. I was scared, I guess. I'd never kissed a girl before. Didn't know what to do with all those feelings. But, Spence, I've always... I've always had a thing for you." She looked up, meeting my eyes. "I just never thought you felt the same way."

I was stunned. "Addison, are you serious? I had no idea. You never—" I stopped, trying to wrap my mind around it. "You never gave any sign."

She laughed softly, reaching for my hand and threading her fingers through mine. "I guess I didn't know how to. But yeah. I used to lie awake at night, wishing you'd kiss me again."

The weight of her words settled over us, and Riley shifted, clearing her throat. "I think we've all got a story like that. I mean, remember that guy I lost it to during *Scream*?" She rolled her eyes, laughing at herself. "Not my finest moment, but it happened."

Addison grinned, her hand still in mine, and nudged Riley. "How could we forget? You wouldn't shut up about it for weeks. Meanwhile, Spence here wouldn't say a word about anything."

I shrugged, the memories washing over me as I took another sip of wine. "What can I say? I didn't want to jinx it. And besides, that's not exactly first-date material."

Riley laughed, and suddenly I found myself wanting to ask the question that had been sitting in the back of my mind for years. "So... who was every-one's first time?"

Addison's cheeks flushed a little, but she didn't shy away. "Well, for me, it was that boy from the soccer team senior year. Thought he was God's gift to the world, but in hindsight, he had no idea what he was doing." She shook her head, smiling a little. "Guess you could say it was underwhelming."

Riley made a face, nodding in agreement. "Mine

was a guy from that band we used to follow around. I don't even remember his name now. But he had a way with words, and I was young and dumb enough to believe every one of them."

I leaned back, listening to their stories, realizing that I'd never really shared mine with them. "Mine was after a night watching *The Notebook*. Romantic as hell, right?" I smirked, thinking back to that moment, the nerves, the clumsy excitement. "But it was awkward. We both thought we knew what we were doing. Spoiler: we didn't. I thought I was never going to find her clit and it was a bit embarrassing."

Addison squeezed my hand, her thumb brushing over my knuckles. "Spence, I wish I'd known. I don't know if I was ever really into those guys. I think I was just looking for something that felt like... well, like this."

The look in her eyes, soft and vulnerable, made my heart ache. I couldn't tell if the wine was making me bold or if it was just years of unsaid words finally bubbling to the surface, but I reached out, tucking a loose strand of hair behind her ear. "Addy, I've thought about that kiss a hundred times. I always wondered what would have happened if I'd just kissed you again."

Riley leaned over, looping her arm around my

shoulders, her voice low. "You still could, you know. We're not fourteen anymore."

Addison laughed, glancing between the two of us. "What are you suggesting, Riley?"

Riley shrugged, her smile a little wicked. "I'm suggesting we stop overthinking it. We've got the wine, the chocolate, the movies... everything we need for a perfect night. Why not see where it takes us?"

The air around us seemed to thrum with tension, each of us caught in the web of old memories and new possibilities. I squeezed Addison's hand, the warmth of Riley's arm around me grounding me as I took a deep breath, feeling like I was standing on the edge of something I'd been waiting for my whole life.

FOUR

T he room was quiet except for the soft hum of the movie, the occasional crackle of popcorn, and the gentle clink of our glasses as we sipped wine under the blankets. We'd piled so many around us that it felt like a cocoon, a little fort where only the three of us existed. I was nestled between Addison and Riley, feeling the comforting warmth of their bodies pressing against mine.

Addison had her arm draped casually over my knee, under the blanket, her fingers resting lightly, almost innocently, against my skin. I thought it might have been accidental until I felt her fingers begin to move, tracing slow circles on my knee. The touch was featherlight, barely there, but enough to send a shiver up my spine. I glanced at her out of the corner of my eye, but she was staring at the screen, her expression calm, almost indifferent.

Riley was laughing at something on the screen, her shoulder nudging mine. I forced myself to join in, to keep my reactions under control, even as Addison's fingers continued their slow, teasing exploration up my thigh. I shifted slightly, testing the waters by parting my legs just a little, a silent signal. Her fingers paused, and I held my breath, waiting.

Then, as if she'd been waiting for my permission, her fingers resumed their journey, moving higher, slipping under the edge of my shorts. I sucked in a breath, fighting to keep my face neutral as a wave of heat washed over me. I could feel my pulse quickening, my heart pounding in my chest as her fingers brushed against my inner thigh.

Addison glanced over at me, her lips curving into a sly smile. She leaned in, her breath warm against my ear. "You okay, Spence?" she murmured, her voice low and teasing.

I managed a nod, though my voice was barely more than a whisper. "Yeah... I'm good." I swallowed hard, trying to ignore the way her fingers were tracing patterns on my skin, slow and deliberate.

Riley turned to us, oblivious, a grin on her face. "This scene always cracks me up," she said, pointing to the screen. "Remember that time we tried to reenact it?"

I forced a laugh, nodding along as if my mind wasn't miles away, focused entirely on the subtle movements of Addison's fingers. I could feel my body reacting, a warm ache settling between my legs, my skin tingling where she touched me.

Addison's hand slipped a little further, her fingers grazing the edge of my panties. I held my breath, my entire body taut with anticipation. She met my eyes, her gaze filled with a heat that sent a thrill through me, and then her fingers dipped beneath the fabric, finding my slickness with unerring accuracy. She began to stroke me slowly, each touch sending a fresh surge of pleasure through me.

I fought to keep my breathing steady, to keep my reactions under control, even as my entire body burned with need. I shifted slightly, opening my legs a little wider, giving her better access, and she took full advantage, her fingers slipping inside, her thumb circling my clit in slow, tantalizing strokes.

Riley was still watching the movie, laughing at something on the screen, completely unaware of what was happening right beside her. The thrill of it, the danger of being caught, only heightened the pleasure, making every touch feel that much more intense.

Addison leaned closer, her breath brushing against my neck as her fingers moved faster, driving me higher. "You're so quiet, Spence," she whispered, her voice a warm, teasing caress against my ear. "Trying to be good?"

I bit down on my lip, fighting to keep the moan from escaping. "I... I don't know if I can," I managed, my voice a ragged whisper.

She chuckled softly, her thumb pressing harder against my clit, pushing me closer and closer to the edge. "Just let go," she murmured, her voice a soothing balm against my growing tension. "I've got you."

Her words washed over me, and I surrendered, my body shuddering as the pleasure peaked, a white-hot wave that left me breathless. I stifled my moan with a cough-laugh, hoping Riley wouldn't notice the flush on my cheeks, the way my fingers gripped the blanket as if it were the only thing keeping me grounded.

Addison's fingers lingered, her touch gentle now, tracing lazy circles that sent aftershocks rippling through me. She leaned back, her hand slipping away, leaving me feeling both satisfied and utterly bereft.

Riley turned to us, a playful smile on her face. "You guys are so quiet. Am I missing something?"

Addison shrugged, a mischievous twinkle in her eye as she glanced at me. "Oh, you know us. Just... enjoying the movie."

Riley laughed, tossing a piece of popcorn at Addison, who caught it with ease. "Yeah, sure. Next time, I want in on whatever secret you two are sharing."

Addison winked at me, her smile conspiratorial. "Don't worry, Riley. I'm sure there's plenty more where that came from."

I felt my cheeks flush again, and I took a long sip of wine, hoping to hide the smile tugging at my lips.

FIVE

T slipped away from the cozy cocoon of blankets and laughter, feeling the need to gather myself. The earlier encounter with Addison had left my mind spinning and my body buzzing, so I wandered into the kitchen, hoping that a snack would steady me. I rummaged through the pantry, reaching for a bag of chips on the top shelf, stretching just enough that my skirt lifted, exposing a sliver of skin to the cool air.

That's when I felt her presence.

"Couldn't resist, could you?" Riley's voice was low, her tone teasing as she leaned against the doorway, watching me with a small smile.

I turned to face her, letting the chips drop back into the cabinet. "Just thought I'd grab something while you two finished the movie." My heart was racing again, the way it always did when she was this close, the way she looked at me with that spark in her eyes.

Riley stepped closer, her gaze slipping from my eyes to my mouth, lingering there for a moment before she met my gaze again. "You don't have to pretend, Spence. I can tell something's on your mind."

I bit my lip, trying to hide the blush creeping up my cheeks. "Maybe you're right."

She moved closer, until there was hardly any space between us, her body radiating warmth. Her hands found my hips, pulling me toward her until I was backed up against the counter, my legs pinned between her and the edge. "You sure it's just snacks you're after?" she murmured, her lips brushing mine in the barest hint of a kiss.

I felt a shiver run through me as her lips grazed mine, a touch so light it was almost a tease. "Maybe not," I whispered, my breath mingling with hers. Before I could think, I leaned in, closing the space between us, pressing my lips to hers.

The kiss was slow at first, exploratory, as if we were both testing the waters, but then Riley's hands tightened on my hips, pulling me closer, and I felt a surge of heat rush through me. She kissed me like she'd been waiting her whole life for this moment, her lips firm and demanding, her tongue tracing the edge of my mouth before slipping inside, teasing mine in a way that made my knees weak.

I reached up, wrapping my arms around her shoulders, pulling her closer as she deepened the kiss. Her hands slipped under the hem of my shirt, her fingers tracing the curve of my waist, sending shivers up my spine. I was barely aware of her lifting me onto the counter until I felt the cool surface beneath me, grounding me even as her touch sent me soaring.

Riley stepped between my legs, her hands resting on my thighs, thumbs tracing slow circles that sent a thrill of anticipation through me. I wrapped my legs around her, pulling her closer, feeling the heat of her body pressing against mine. She broke the kiss, trailing her lips down my neck, leaving a path of warmth in her wake.

"You're so beautiful," she murmured against my skin, her voice soft, almost reverent. Her hands wandered, slipping beneath my dress, pushing it up as she kissed her way down my chest, her lips brushing over my collarbone, my skin tingling in the wake of her touch.

I tilted my head back, my breath coming in shallow gasps as her hands moved over me, her touch gentle yet insistent. I felt a strange sense of urgency, a hunger that I hadn't realized I was capable of, and I pulled her closer, needing to feel her, to have her as close as possible.

Her gaze dropped to the counter beside me, and she picked up a cucumber with a playful grin. "You know," she said, holding it up between us, "I've always wondered..."

I let out a breathless laugh, my cheeks flushing with anticipation as I nodded, giving her permission. She moved back, her gaze never leaving mine as she slowly slid the cucumber between my legs, pressing it against my hot, wet, center, testing my reaction.

The coolness of it sent a shock through me, and I gasped, my fingers gripping the edge of the counter as she began to move, her touch gentle yet firm. She watched me closely, her eyes filled with a mixture of curiosity and desire as she pushed it deeper, her movements slow and deliberate, drawing out every reaction, every shiver and moan.

I felt my body tense, the pleasure building in slow, relentless waves, each movement of her hand bringing me closer to the edge. My breath was coming in short gasps, my body on fire as she worked me, her eyes dark with intensity as she watched me fall apart beneath her touch.

Riley leaned in, her lips brushing mine as she

whispered, "You're so responsive, Spence. I could watch you like this forever."

Her words sent a fresh surge of heat through me, and I felt myself tipping over the edge, my body shuddering as the pleasure peaked, a wave of ecstasy washing over me that left me breathless and trembling. I clung to her, my nails digging into her shoulders as I rode out the high, feeling like I was floating, lost in a sea of sensation.

When I finally came back to earth, Riley was there, steadying me, her hands gentle as she lowered me back onto the counter. She knelt between my legs, her mouth finding my center, tasting me with a reverence that made my heart ache. Her tongue was soft, gentle, drawing out the last shudders of pleasure as she held me close, her hands gripping my thighs as if she couldn't bear to let me go.

I leaned back, my head resting against the cabinet, my body spent and sated, feeling like I'd just been through something transformative, something that had changed me in ways I couldn't quite understand. Riley stood, her gaze meeting mine with a satisfied smile, and she leaned in, pressing a gentle kiss to my lips.

"I've wanted to do that for so long," she

murmured, her fingers brushing a stray strand of hair from my face.

I reached up, pulling her close, my heart swelling with a mix of gratitude and desire. "Me too," I whispered, my voice barely more than a breath, but she heard me, and her smile widened, her eyes bright with joy.

CHAPTER
SIX

I woke to the smell of bacon and the sound of laughter drifting down the hall. Sunlight streamed through the window, warming the room as I blinked the sleep from my eyes. The memories of the night before flooded back in a wave, and I couldn't help the smile that crept across my face as I rolled out of bed, slipping on a shirt before heading toward the kitchen.

As I reached the doorway, I paused, taking in the scene. Riley and Addison were dancing around the kitchen, spatulas in hand, the music turned up as they twirled and laughed, flipping pancakes and stirring eggs. I watched them for a moment, a sense of warmth filling my chest. This was home. This was where I belonged.

Addison spotted me first, breaking into a grin.

"Look who decided to join us!" she called, flipping a pancake with an exaggerated flourish.

"Morning, sleepyhead!" Riley added, nudging me with her hip as I joined them at the counter. "We're making the ultimate breakfast feast. Pancakes, bacon, eggs... the works."

I laughed, grabbing a knife and a bowl of fresh strawberries from the fridge. "Guess I'll be on fruit duty, then," I said, starting to slice the strawberries as I fell into the familiar rhythm of our friendship.

They continued to dance around the kitchen as they cooked, adding scrambled eggs and sausage to the growing pile of food on the counter. I cut up strawberries, pineapple, and melon, the scents mingling in a heady mix that made my stomach rumble with anticipation.

We carried everything over to the table, loading up our plates with pancakes smothered in syrup, crispy bacon, and fresh fruit. As we settled in, Addison glanced over at me, her eyes sparkling with mischief. "Do you remember when we used to have those 'Newsies' parties?"

I couldn't help but laugh, nodding as the memories washed over me. "Oh my gods, yes. We watched that movie every weekend for, what, five years straight?"

Riley groaned, rolling her eyes. "I'm pretty sure

we could still recite every line if we tried. We were obsessed."

"Newsies every Friday and Saturday night," Addison chimed in, grinning. "We'd quote the lines, dance around the room... I think we even tried to learn the choreography at one point."

"Of course we did," I replied, chuckling as I remembered our high school selves, giddy with excitement as we watched the same scenes over and over, staying up until the early hours of the morning. "We must've driven our parents crazy."

Riley smirked, raising her glass of orange juice in a mock toast. "To our poor, long-suffering parents. They put up with a lot."

We clinked glasses, laughing as we reminisced, the years melting away as we recounted the silly things we'd done together—sleepovers that stretched into whole weekends, midnight snack runs, and the time we'd stayed up until dawn trying to catch the sunrise, only to fall asleep minutes before it happened.

As we finished breakfast, Addison glanced over at me, a playful glint in her eyes. "You know, there's one thing we haven't done in a while."

I raised an eyebrow, grinning. "Oh? And what's that?"

"Truth or dare," she replied, a mischievous smile

spreading across her face. "Come on, it's been forever since we played. And after last night... I think it could get interesting."

I glanced at Riley, who was already nodding, a similar sparkle in her eyes. "I'm game," she said, her voice laced with anticipation.

I shrugged, leaning back in my chair. "Alright, I'm in. Who's going first?"

Addison sat up straighter, looking between the two of us. "I'll go first. Spencer—truth or dare?"

I hesitated for a moment, then decided to start simple. "Truth."

She leaned in, her gaze piercing as she asked, "What's the one sexual fantasy you've always wanted to try but never have?"

I felt a blush creeping up my neck, but I met her gaze, the playful energy between us emboldening me. "I've always wanted to try... public sex. Like, somewhere risky, where we could get caught." I took a breath, feeling a thrill rush through me as I confessed, but Addison and Riley only exchanged glances, their eyes lighting up with shared excitement.

Riley grinned, clearly enjoying my answer. "Interesting... we'll have to keep that in mind." She winked at me, sending a shiver through my spine.

Then she turned to Addison. "Alright, Addy—truth or dare?"

Addison grinned, her eyes narrowing. "Dare. Let's make it interesting."

Riley thought for a moment, a slow smile spreading across her face. "I dare you to... kiss Spencer. Like you mean it."

Addison didn't hesitate. She leaned over, cupping my face with one hand as she brought her lips to mine. The kiss was slow and sensual, deepening as her hand slid to the back of my neck, pulling me closer. I could feel my heart racing as her tongue teased mine, her lips soft but insistent, leaving me breathless by the time she pulled away.

I opened my eyes to find Riley watching us, her expression hungry as she licked her lips. "Wow," she murmured, her voice barely more than a whisper. "That was... something."

Addison smirked, wiping her thumb over my bottom lip. "Your turn, Spence. Truth or dare?"

My pulse was still racing from the kiss, and I felt a surge of courage. "Dare."

She glanced at Riley, a wicked grin spreading across her face. "I dare you to give Riley a lap dance."

Riley raised an eyebrow, looking more than a little intrigued. "Well, I'm not going to say no to that."

Laughing, I stood up, taking Riley's hand and pulling her onto the couch. The music played softly in the background as I straddled her lap, moving my hips in time with the beat, feeling her hands settle on my waist. Her eyes were dark with desire as I leaned in, trailing my hands over her shoulders, arching my back as I moved against her, every touch, every look between us charged with an electricity that left me breathless.

When I finally pulled away, I sat back down, my skin flushed, my body humming with anticipation. Riley took a deep breath, looking at me like she was trying to memorize every inch of me.

Addison broke the silence, grinning as she leaned back. "Riley, truth or dare?"

"Truth," she replied, her gaze never leaving mine.

Addison leaned forward, her voice low. "What's the most intimate thing you've ever wanted to do with one of us?"

Riley hesitated, glancing between us before she spoke, her voice barely more than a whisper. "I've always wanted to... tie Spencer up. Explore her body. Take my time."

My breath caught, and I felt a surge of heat rush through me, a potent mixture of excitement and longing that seemed to pulse between us. This game

—what had started as playful dares and teasing questions—was stripping away the last remnants of distance, exposing all the emotions that we had once kept safely hidden. Every truth revealed, every touch shared, seemed to dissolve another barrier until there was nothing left between us but raw, honest vulnerability. I looked at them both, feeling their presence like a tangible warmth, the love and desire in their eyes mirroring my own.

Addison's fingers intertwined with mine, her grip firm and reassuring, while Riley reached over to tuck a strand of hair behind my ear, her touch lingering. In that moment, I realized just how deeply connected we were, how much we had always been, even if we had never dared to fully admit it. We were bound by years of memories, laughter, and shared secrets, and now, finally, by the unspoken emotions that had hovered between us for so long. It felt like all the pieces were finally falling into place, and I could barely breathe from the intensity of it.

We continued the game, each question and each dare drawing us closer, the boundaries between friendship and something more blurring beyond recognition. I could feel the walls around my heart softening, dissolving with every whispered confession and lingering touch. Addison and Riley looked at me with an openness that was both thrilling and terrifying, their eyes filled with promises and possibilities.

By the time we finished, we were tangled together on the couch, our bodies draped over one another like we were trying to merge into a single being. The room was filled with the sound of our quiet laughter, the echoes of our confessions hanging in the air like a gentle reminder of all we'd shared. The first light of morning filtered through the window, casting a soft glow over us, and I felt cocooned in the warmth of their presence, surrounded by a love that was deep, abiding, and impossibly tender.

As I lay there between them, basking in the afterglow of our game, I realized that this was what it meant to truly come home. It wasn't just the memories or the laughter or the familiar touch—it was the way they saw me, completely, and still wanted to stay. I closed my eyes, letting the feeling wash over me, knowing that no matter what came next, I would always have this. I would always have them.

SEVEN

After breakfast, the three of us collapsed back onto the couch, feeling sated and content, and decided to put on another movie. We ended up playing rock-paper-scissors to see who'd be the unlucky one to leave our cozy nest and pick up lunch. Luck wasn't on my side this time.

"Alright, alright," I groaned, slipping into my shoes. "I'll go grab us some food. You two better not finish this movie without me!"

They waved me off with matching grins, and I made my way out the door, stepping into the warmth of the midday sun. The town was quiet, a gentle breeze rustling through the trees as I strolled down the familiar streets. On a whim, I decided to stop by Spellbound Stories. I'd been meaning to grab a particular book for a while now, and I figured it was as good a time as any.

The bell above the door chimed as I stepped inside, inhaling the comforting scent of books and a hint of lavender from the candles burning on the counter. I scanned the aisles, my eyes landing on Lea, the store's owner, who was busy rearranging a shelf of hardcovers. She looked up as I approached, a warm smile lighting up her face.

"Spencer! It's been a while," she greeted, brushing a strand of red hair behind her ear. Lea was striking—tall and effortlessly sexy, with a confidence that had always intrigued me. Her gaze lingered on me, and I felt a familiar thrill run through me.

"It has," I replied, stepping closer. "I've missed stopping by. You look as gorgeous as ever, Lea."

Her smile widened, and she arched an eyebrow. "Well, aren't you sweet? What brings you in today?"

I leaned against the shelf, meeting her gaze with a grin. "I came for a book, but now that I'm here... I'm thinking I'd rather have my way with you between the shelves."

Her eyes sparkled with mischief, and she took a step closer, closing the distance between us. "Is that so?" she murmured, her voice a low purr that made my pulse quicken.

Before I could respond, the door chimed again, and I turned to see Alex, Lea's husband, striding into the store. He was ruggedly handsome, with an easy charm and a smile that seemed to always be at the ready. He walked over to Lea, pressing a kiss to her cheek before turning to me with a grin.

"Spencer! Good to see you. Which book has got you stopping by?"

Lea shot me a sly glance before turning to Alex. "Spencer here is looking for a new experience," she said, her tone laced with innuendo as she winked at him.

Alex's grin widened, and he raised an eyebrow. "Oh? What kind of experience are we talking about?"

Lea leaned in, whispering something in his ear that I couldn't quite catch, but whatever she said made him chuckle, his eyes gleaming with excitement. He looked back at me, his gaze appraising. "Well, now... that does sound interesting."

I felt a blush creep up my cheeks, realizing the situation I'd walked myself into. "Oh, I was just... I mean, I didn't mean to—"

Lea cut me off with a laugh, placing a hand on my arm. "Spence, don't backpedal now. You've piqued my interest." She glanced over at Alex, sharing a silent conversation, their expressions speaking volumes. "What do you say, love? Should we give her a little adventure?"

Alex grinned, nodding. "I think we should. But only if I get to watch."

My heart skipped a beat, and I felt a rush of excitement. "You mean... really?"

Lea moved closer, her eyes locking onto mine. "Absolutely. I've always wanted to do this," she murmured, taking my hand and leading me toward the back of the store, where the aisles were hidden from view. Alex followed, his gaze steady and filled with anticipation.

Once we were tucked away in a secluded corner, Lea leaned against the shelf, pulling me toward her. "Someone could walk in at any moment," she whispered, her voice filled with a delicious tension. "Doesn't that turn you on, Spence?"

I bit my lip, nodding as I felt the familiar thrill of excitement surge through me. "You have no idea," I replied, my voice barely more than a breath.

She closed the distance between us, pressing her lips to mine with a hunger that made my knees weak. I wrapped my arms around her, pulling her close as our kiss deepened, my hands exploring the curve of her waist, the warmth of her skin beneath her shirt. Her body pressed against mine, pinning me to the shelf as we lost ourselves in the kiss, our breaths mingling, our hearts racing.

Lea broke away, her lips trailing down my neck, her hands slipping under my shirt as she pulled it up, exposing my skin to the cool air. I shivered as she leaned down, taking one of my breasts into her mouth, her tongue tracing circles around my nipple, making it harden beneath her touch. I gasped, gripping the edge of the shelf as she continued her exploration, her mouth leaving a trail of heat in its wake.

Out of the corner of my eye, I saw Alex watching us, his eyes dark with desire, his lips parted as he took in every detail. I met his gaze, feeling a new surge of excitement at the way he watched, his expression a mix of admiration and longing.

Lea's hands moved lower, finding the waistband of my skirt, and she glanced up at me, her eyes filled with a question. I nodded, giving her permission, and she slipped her hand beneath the fabric, her fingers finding my center, already wet with anticipation. She began to move, her touch gentle but insistent, sending waves of pleasure through me as she worked me with practiced skill.

I closed my eyes, letting the sensation wash over me, feeling my body respond to her every touch, every movement. I could hear Alex's breath quicken, and the sound only heightened the experience, adding a new layer of excitement to the already charged atmosphere.

Lea's fingers moved faster, her other hand gripping my hip as she brought me closer and closer to the edge. I could feel the tension building, my body tightening as I hovered on the brink, and then, with a final push, I came, a shuddering wave of pleasure that left me breathless and trembling in her arms.

As I came down from the high, I felt Lea's lips on mine once more, soft and gentle, a contrast to the intensity of our encounter. Alex moved closer, pressing a kiss to Lea's cheek, his hand resting on her shoulder as he looked at me with a satisfied smile.

"Lea's been wanting to do that for a while now," he murmured, his voice filled with warmth. "This was my gift to her."

I smiled, feeling a deep sense of gratitude and connection as I took in the two of them, standing there together, their love for each other as clear as the desire we'd just shared. In that moment, I felt like I'd found something rare and beautiful.

EIGHT

As I left Spellbound Stories, a smile played on my lips, and I felt a surge of confidence. My body still hummed with the remnants of my encounter with Lea and Alex, and my mind replayed every delicious moment. I felt alive, like a version of myself I'd always wanted to be but had only just discovered. The sun was bright overhead, and the world seemed to pulse with energy, as if I'd been given some secret that only I could understand.

I continued down the street, my stride easy, savoring the way people glanced my way, almost as if they could sense the change in me. I was drawn to the bright red sign of Golden Chopsticks, the smell of stir-fried vegetables and spices drifting out as I reached for the door.

But as soon as my hand touched the door handle, the world spun around me, and suddenly, I wasn't standing on the street anymore. I was back in the Arcane Room, lying on the chaise lounge, blinking up at the ceiling as if I'd just woken from a dream.

"Ah, you're back," came Ms. Vesper's familiar voice, warm and steady. She was seated at the foot of the couch, her legs crossed, watching me with a knowing smile. "How are you feeling?"

I sat up slowly, glancing around the room, my heart pounding as I tried to make sense of it. "Wait... so it was all...?"

She nodded, her smile widening. "Yes. Everything you experienced was part of the journey brought on by the tea and the Three of Cups."

I took a deep breath, the memories flooding back with an almost overwhelming intensity. "It felt so real," I murmured, running a hand through my hair. "The night with my friends, the coffee shop, the bookstore... every single moment felt real."

Ms. Vesper leaned forward, her gaze kind. "That's the magic of the Arcane Room. It brings out the desires, the emotions you carry with you, and helps you explore them in a way that feels tangible and safe. You experienced what you needed to experience."

I met her eyes, a wave of gratitude washing over me. "It's like... I feel more myself than I ever have. Like I've uncovered something I didn't even know was missing."

Ms. Vesper nodded, her smile gentle. "The Three of Cups is about connection, celebration, and self-discovery. You've always had that strength within you, Spencer. This journey simply allowed you to see it, to embody it, without the weight of everyday life holding you back."

I took a moment to reflect on her words, letting them sink in. Everything I'd felt over the course of that night—the love, the desire, the freedom—had left an indelible mark on me. I'd always known I cared deeply for Addison and Riley, but now I saw our connection with new clarity. And the experiences with the women I'd encountered along the way had shown me a new side of myself, one that was confident and unafraid to embrace what she wanted.

"I feel... liberated," I said, the words surprising me even as I spoke them. "Like I'm not afraid anymore. I'm ready to go after what I want, to be who I want to be."

Ms. Vesper's eyes twinkled with approval. "That's exactly what I hoped you would find. The Arcane Room offers the path, but you walk it."

I took a deep breath, feeling a sense of fulfillment that resonated deeply within me. "Thank you," I murmured, the words filled with a quiet gratitude. "I don't think I'll ever look at life the same way again."

Ms. Vesper stood, moving to the door, her movements graceful and fluid. "Remember, Spencer, the magic of the Three of Cups is with you, even outside the Arcane Room. You carry it with you in every connection you make, in every truth you embrace. It's not something you leave behind."

As I stood to join her, I felt a weight lift from my shoulders, a sense of lightness that I hadn't realized I'd been missing. I turned to face her, feeling the warmth of her presence and the wisdom she'd shared. "I'll hold onto that," I promised, a smile tugging at the corners of my lips. "It's time I started living the way I always dreamed I could."

With a nod, Ms. Vesper opened the door, and I stepped out into the world again, feeling as if I was seeing it for the first time. The town looked the same, but I knew that I'd changed. I'd been given a glimpse of my deepest desires, my truest self, and I wasn't about to let that go.

I'd found my way home to myself, and there was nothing that could take that away from me.

. . .

Sɪɢɴ up for Jax Wilder's newsletter and receive a collection of unpublished Coral Cove short stories. Meet familiar characters and dive deeper into the love and romance that Coral Cove is known for. Don't miss out on this exclusive content!

https://mailchi.mp/158597581671/jax-wilder

Jax Wilder

If you enjoyed the *3 of Cups*, I hope you'll check out *Dawning Desire* in my Coral Cove series.

Sᴀᴘᴘʜɪᴄ ʟᴏᴠᴇ, **divine desire, cosmic passion.**

Lɪʟʟʏ

I was betrothed.

I was never supposed to fall in love with beauty as radiant as the moonlight itself.

But we fell in love anyway.

The gods cursed my love to live as a human for ten-thousand years.

She forgets who I am over and over and over.

So, I have to reminder her.

OPHELIA

She took my books.

Then she took my breath.

I can't shake the feeling that I've known her before.

Maybe in another life.

But I don't have time for love while I'm trying to make partner.

COSMIC LOVE, destined passion, irresistible desire.

TAI-YANG, goddess of the sun, has always followed the celestial laws. Destined to be with Hou Yi, the famed archer of the skies, her fate seemed certain— until she met Luna, the goddess of the moon. Their forbidden connection burned brighter than the stars, and in their love, Tai-Yang found something worth defying the gods for.

But love between goddesses comes with consequences. Banished to Earth and reincarnated over centuries, Luna forgets Tai-Yang with every new life. Yet during a rare eclipse, memories return for a fleeting moment, reigniting the passion and love between them. Will they break the gods' curse or face eternal separation?

Dawning Desire is a heart-pounding FF romance that blends mythological elements, forbidden love, and cosmic passion. Perfect for fans of sapphic romance and powerful goddesses defying destiny.

Also by Jax Wilder

Coral Cove Series

Sleighed by Love

Harvesting Love

Dawning Desire

Knead You Now

Love Rewound

Perfect Lover Spell

Haunted by Her

Red, White, and Ravished

Tarot Fantasies Series

The Devil's Temptations

Strength of the Beast

Hanged Passions

Six of Cups

Death's Embrace

Queen of Pentacles

Seven of Pentacles

Ace of Wands

Three of Swords

Lovers In The Veil

<u>Two of Swords</u>

Coastal Cupid Series

HeartBound Souls

Fae Ring Series

Alice and Her Mad Hatters

Stand Alone Titles

Pride and Prejudice and Witches

Additional Books by

Rainbow Quartz Publishing

Lorelai Hamilton

Encyclopedia of Divination

Encyclopedia of Cryptids

Encyclopedia of Faeries

Tarot Tales and Magic Spells

Teenage Tarot

Arcane In Verse

The Eclectic Witch's Grimoire

Teenage Witch's Grimoire

Find Your Bliss

Tarot Reflection Journal

Tarot Refection Journal Coloring The Tarot

Dream Journal

Miranda Levi

From A Youth A Fountain Did Flow

The Sea Withdrew

A Tear In Time

Mo(ther) Na(ture)

In Orion's Hands

Jackson Anhalt

From The 911 Files

Isla Watts

A Fairy Bad Day

Surprise! You're a Vampire

Gorgeous, Gorgeous, Gorgons

Mork The Handsome Orc

Adopted By Werewolves

Bite Me If You Can

That's The Spirit!

Rose Dawson's Book Journals

My Time With The Fairies

Enchanted Escapades

Enchanted Escapades

Dewey Decimal Diaries

Siren's Songbook

Pride and Prejudice

Bibliophile's Bounty

Book of Books Journal

Pages & Passages Reading Journal

Bookworm's Companion Reading Journal & Tracker

ABOUT THE AUTHOR

Jax Wilder is a passionate romance author hailing from a charming small town nestled in the picturesque Pacific Northwest. With a heart full of love and an unyielding belief in the power of happily ever afters, Jax weaves enchanting tales of love and connection that leave readers captivated.

Jax's novels are a reflection of her commitment to celebrating the magic of love, and her characters' journeys mirror the warmth and happiness she has found in her own life. Join her on the enchanting journey of love, passion, and enduring connection through her heartfelt romance novels.